D0810394

NOT-SO-
WEIRD
Emma

SaLLy WARNER

Illustrated by

jamie HARPER

PUFFIN BOOKS

PUFFIN BOOKS
Published by the Penguin Group
Penguin Young Readers Group, 345 Hudson Street, New York, New York 10014, U.S.A.
Penguin Group (Canada), 90 Eglinton Avenue East, Suite 700,
Toronto, Ontario, Canada M4P 2Y3 (a division of Pearson Penguin Canada Inc.)
Penguin Books Ltd, 80 Strand, London WC2R 0RL, England
Penguin Ireland, 25 St Stephen's Green, Dublin 2, Ireland
(a division of Penguin Books Ltd)
Penguin Group (Australia), 250 Camberwell Road, Camberwell, Victoria 3124, Australia
(a division of Pearson Australia Group Pty Ltd)
Penguin Books India Pvt Ltd, 11 Community Centre,
Panchsheel Park, New Delhi - 110 017, India
Penguin Group (NZ), 67 Apollo Drive, Mairangi Bay, Auckland 1311, New Zealand
(a division of Pearson New Zealand Ltd)
Penguin Books (South Africa) (Pty) Ltd, 24 Sturdee Avenue,
Rosebank, Johannesburg 2196, South Africa

Registered Offices: Penguin Books Ltd, 80 Strand, London WC2R 0RL, England

First published in the United States of America by Viking,
a division of Penguin Young Readers Group, 2005
Published by Puffin Books, a division of Penguin Young Readers Group, 2007

3 5 7 9 10 8 6 4 2

Text copyright © Sally Warner, 2005
Illustrations copyright © Jamie Harper, 2005
All rights reserved

THE LIBRARY OF CONGRESS HAS CATALOGED THE VIKING EDITION AS FOLLOWS:
Warner, Sally.
Not-So-Weird Emma / by Sally Warner; illustrated by Jamie Harper.
p. cm.
Summary: Eight-year-old Emma is just beginning to like her new school when her
friend Cynthia starts telling other kids that Emma is, well, a little strange.
ISBN: 0-670-06005-4 (hardcover)
[1. First day of school—Fiction. 2. Schools—Fiction.
3. Friendship—Fiction.] I. Harper, Jamie, ill. II. Title.
PZ7.W24644We 2005
[Fic]—dc22 2004028986
Set in Bitstream Carmina
Book design by Nancy Brennan

Puffin Books ISBN 978-0-14-240807-0

Printed in the United States of America

For the wonderful Katherine Brophy! —S. W.

x x x

For Mary and Marty—J. H.

CONTEN

x 1 x
ᴀʀᴇ ʏᴏᴜ Lɪsᴛᴇɴɪɴɢ?

"Settle down," Ms. Sanchez calls out as we straggle into the classroom. She claps her hands once, and her engagement ring flashes. You should see it.

You can tell that she means business. Everyone sits down fast, as if we are playing a game of musical chairs. I sit down fast, too. There is a scuffle over by the window. "Ow. Quit it," Annie Pat says to Jared Matthews. She rubs the top part of her arm.

I secretly call Jared "Jar-Head," because he is so mean to little kids, especially the ones in kindergarten and first grade. Just because we are in third grade doesn't mean we have to be bullies, does it? Also, his mud-brown guinea-pig swirly hair always looks as though he has been sleeping on it—or as though an invisible lid was just twisted off his head. He is the biggest kid in my class.

My name is Emma McGraw. I am the second littlest kid in class, next to EllRay Jakes. EllRay is small in size but large in noise.

Jared holds up both of his square hands and makes his eyes big and round to show how innocent he is. "It was an accident," he says. But he is making sure that the other boys—especially Kevin, EllRay, and Corey—see that he is laughing at Annie Pat.

"I have an announcement to make," Ms. Sanchez says. Her eyes are sparkling. It must be a good announcement, not a bad one, like *Uh-oh*, *you all have to take home this letter to your parents about head lice*, or a confusing one, like *Guess what? The P.T.A. is having another candy sale, even though everyone keeps telling you not to eat candy.*

Fish hide in coral reefs to catch food.

The entire third-grade class wriggles with excitement at the same time. Even the chairs look more alert. It reminds me of this nature show I saw once on the Animal Planet about a coral reef. The whole reef was alive, every little part of it.

See, that's what's so great about nature: the interesting surprises. In real life, the surprises are all the kind of thing that makes you feel sick to your stomach—like when your mom loses her job, and you have to move from a house to a condo, and you have to transfer from one school to another for practically no reason at all. Just because of someone not making enough money to pay private school tuition anymore.

"Emma McGraw, are you listening?" Ms. Sanchez asks.

Uh-oh. My new friend Cynthia Harbison looks down at her hands, embarrassed for me. Jared snickers, and Corey blushes, but I nod and look alert. "Yes, I'm listening," I say.

"Well, good," Ms. Sanchez says, smiling, "because I don't want anyone to miss what I have to say." She looks around for a second, still smiling. It's as though she wants us to love her for what she hasn't even announced yet.

Someone sneezes, and everyone laughs. Sneezes are always funny in our class. I don't know why.

"Now, I know that school only started a few weeks ago," Ms. Sanchez says, "but you've all been working pretty hard. And I know that some of you have been struggling."

Next to me, I hear Corey Robinson give a little groan. I think he is allergic to arithmetic.

" . . . so I've planned a treat for all you third-graders," Ms. Sanchez is saying.

Heather's hand shoots up in the air, as usual. She holds her arm up with her other hand, as if otherwise it might fall off. "Oh, oh," she says, before Ms. Sanchez has even called on her. "Are we going on a field trip? Because my big sister's class, they went on a field trip to the San Diego Zoo, in a bus."

A trip to the zoo! I'm glad that I am paying attention now. I have been to the zoo a lot of times with my mom, of course, but this would be different. This would be official. It would be like we were real nature scientists, almost—traveling on a special research bus.

7

And a nature scientist is what I want to be when I grow up.

"No, it's not the zoo," Ms. Sanchez says, and my hopes drop right down into my shoes. "And it's not any kind of a field trip," she continues. "The treat will be right here, this Friday, on our very own playground. Well, on the lawn next to the playground."

I hide my fingers and start counting on them, even though I have supposedly outgrown doing this. Today is Tuesday, so my fingers tell me that the surprise will happen in three more days.

"Our treat will happen right after lunch," Ms. Sanchez says in a singsong, keeping-secrets kind of voice. "Now, be sure to wear play clothes on Friday, and not your usual prom dresses and dinner jackets," she teases us. "And tell your moms and dads," she adds. "They are welcome to join us, if they can take a little time off work. And they might want to bring their cameras."

"We don't have to wear costumes, do we?"

Jared asks, sounding suspicious. "Are you going to make us put on funny hats or have a parade?" It is only October, but I know already that Jared is not a parade kind of kid. And if there was ever a Funny Hat Day at this school, he would stay home with a convenient stomach ache or something.

I'm sure of it.

Ms. Sanchez laughs out loud. "No, don't worry, Jared. You're safe."

"Because I'm not wearing any funny hat," Jared announces.

I guess he thinks having funny hair is bad enough. Funny hats would be too much.

"No hats," Ms. Sanchez promises. "Friday will be a hat-free day, okay?"

Heather's hand flies up again. "Oh, oh," she says. "And no coconut, okay? Because I get a rash."

"Oh, darn," Ms. Sanchez cries, pretending to be disappointed. She slaps her desk with her left hand, and the ring makes rainbow shines. "The treat was going to be that you would all eat coconuts while wearing silly costumes and hats and then have a parade. And now it's *ruined*."

Heather starts to pout. "I was only saying," she mutters. She looks around for sympathy, but everyone is too busy whispering to notice her.

"Now get out your workbooks," Ms. Sanchez calls out. "It's time to do some heavy-duty subtraction."

Poor Corey groans again.

I guess it's back to real life—until Friday afternoon, anyway.

x 2 x

a Lizard eating a Grasshopper

The kick ball bounces up and bonks me in the leg at recess when I am right in the middle of a daydream. I pick it up and try to figure out where to throw it. Corey Robinson and Jared Matthews are both holding up their hands. "Give it here," Jared shouts at me. I pretend that I am trying to, but really I throw it to Corey. Corey has a million freckles, and they all seem to leap up to catch the ball.

"Sorry," I say to Jared, shrugging a little bit.

"*Grrr,*" Jared says back at me, and he turns to run after Corey.

I take a deep breath and walk over to the chain-link fence, where Cynthia Harbison, Heather, and Annie Pat are hanging out. I try to look as though I don't care what happens once I get there, even though I am feeling a little funny.

See, this is my first year at Oak Glen Primary School. I used to go to Magdalena School, which is girls only. It was in another part of Oak Glen, which is the name of the town we live in. Oak Glen is in California, about an hour away from San Diego. But we're in the hills, not on the ocean.

So yes, I am the new kid in the third grade at Oak Glen, and that makes me feel like an outsider. That is why it is hard for me to make new friends, I guess. Friends other than Cynthia, I mean—and Cynthia seems to like it that way. She wants to be the only friend I have, in other words, but she is with two other girls, now. And so who knows what will happen?

Here is something confusing: Cynthia Harbison has lots of friends, even though she is crabby. I only have one friend, Cynthia. She dropped her shiny pink notebook the first day of class, and I helped her picked it up. After that, she kind of adopted me.

My mom tries to make me feel better about not having lots of friends at Oak Glen. She says that it is only the beginning of October, after all, and I will make other friends by the end of the school year.

A hundred years from now.

Huh, that's easy for her to say. So far, it's only Cynthia—and sometimes I don't even like *her* very much.

I reach the fence where the girls are standing and hook one of my fingers through a link. I imagine myself climbing over the fence like a monkey and escaping to freedom. "Hi, Emma," Annie Pat says. She has bouncy red hair, and blushes whenever Ms. Sanchez calls on her. Annie Pat is nice to me sometimes, but I don't know her very well—*yet*.

"Oh, hi," I say to Annie Pat, as if I am kind of surprised to see her standing there.

Heather leans over and whispers something in Cynthia's ear, and they both laugh. Shade from the eucalyptus tree flickers across Heather's face.

"Jared Matthews yelled at you, Emma," Heather says, looking serious and excited at the same time. "You'd better watch out."

"Emma doesn't care," Cynthia says, teasing. "She's not scared. Are you, Emma?"

"Nuh-uh," I lie.

Heather and Cynthia look at each other quick as a flash of lightning. "Then why don't you go kick the ball around with those boys, if you're so brave?" Heather says, aiming a mean smile in my direction.

"She probably could if she wanted to," Annie Pat says, sounding proud of me, for some mysterious reason. "She just doesn't want to."

"Yeah," I say, my heart thumping. "I guess I could if I wanted to. But what's so great about playing kick ball with a bunch of boys?"

Now Cynthia frowns. I guess she doesn't like Annie Pat sticking up for me, but who knows why?

"You're not that good a runner," Heather tells

me. "You'd probably get hurt if you tried to play with the boys."

"I am too a good runner," I say.

"She is," Annie Pat says, nodding. "I saw her once."

Cynthia scowls even more.

Heather shrugs. "Well anyway, I was only joking," she says. "Girls don't play the same games on the playground that the boys do. Not at *this* school," she adds, giving me a dirty look—as if it's my fault I used to go someplace else.

(Thanks a lot, Mom.)

"But Emma could play kick ball if she wanted to," Annie Pat says again, sticking up for me.

This is too much for Cynthia, I guess. I can tell that by the look on her face, which is saying, *Hey, Emma McGraw is my friend, not yours!* "Go ahead and play, then, Emma," Cynthia says out loud. She turns back to Heather, as though she wants to explain something. "Emma doesn't

mind being kind of weird," she says. "You should
see her bedroom."

My bedroom.

I can't believe what I am hearing.

It's true that Cynthia has slept over at our
new condo a couple of times, but my bedroom is
perfectly normal, in my opinion. Anyway, if

crabby Cynthia is mad at Annie Pat, why is she picking on *me*?

"Why?" Heather says, grinning and twinkling. "What's so weird about Emma's bedroom?"

Annie Pat looks worried now.

"It's all covered with nature posters," Cynthia says, as if she has just described something truly disgusting—but that she knows her listeners will enjoy hearing. "It's just like being in a *boy's* room," she adds.

I can feel my face get hot, and I instantly wish I were not wearing the overalls and T-shirt that I thought looked so comfortable this morning. Because who cares about being comfortable? I look like Dennis the Menace!

I look like a boy, if you don't count my hair.

"That's not true, Cynthia," I say in a shaky voices. "And anyway, how would you know what a boy's room looks like? You don't have any brothers."

"Are you saying Cynthia is lying?" Heather

asks me, raising one eyebrow in disbelief. "You *don't* have nature posters all over the walls?"

"No," I say. "I mean, I do. But it's not like a boy's room. Anyone could like nature. Even supermodels like nature. I've seen them talk about it on TV."

"She's got fish and dolphins and sharks and whales and stuff on one wall," Cynthia reports, her eyes glittering. "Then she's got pictures of land animals all over another wall. Even the not-cute ones like hyenas. I hate to say this, but Emma is kind of strange."

Like I said before, I cannot believe what I am hearing! Cynthia kept asking and *asking* to come over to my house, and we played and everything—and all the time, she was looking at my walls, thinking how strange they were?

And now she's *telling* everyone? No fair!

I feel so embarrassed that I don't know where to look.

"That doesn't sound so bad," Annie Pat says,

trying to stick up for me. "I like nature, too. I have some pictures of baby animals on my closet door, as a matter of fact. They're so darling."

I want to tell her to be quiet, or she will only make everything worse.

Too late. "Yeah," Cynthia is saying, "except that Emma collects the really creepy stuff. Like, she has tons of snakes and frogs and lizards up on *her* walls. There's even this one picture of a lizard eating a grasshopper. And the poor little grasshopper's legs are sticking right out of the lizard's mouth. You can practically see them kicking."

"Eeew, that is so messed up," Heather squeals.

Well, lizards have to eat, too. What did Cynthia think, that they would just use the drive-through window at Burger King when their little green stomachs started to growl?

But even Annie Pat seems to be kind of grossed out, hearing about the grasshopper and the lizard. She gives me a pitying look, which I wish I could grab hold of and shove right back at her.

Bonk! The red kick ball hits my leg again, on purpose this time—and it's just when the bell rings, too. "Ha ha," Jared laughs. "The ball touched you last, so you're the one who has to bring it in," he shouts at me.

He's right. That's the stupid rule at this stupid school.

And so Cynthia, Heather, and Annie Pat get to walk slowly back to class, while I have to scramble after the kick ball. It skitters away from me like a bad little dog that doesn't want to be caught.

Cynthia and Heather put their heads together and whisper on their way out of the playground. Annie Pat gives me a sad look over her shoulder.

And I feel like crying.

"Come on, Emma. Shake your tail feathers," Ms. Sanchez calls out, standing by the gate. She is holding a giant blue net bag that bulges with recess balls.

I finally pounce on the escaped kick ball and capture it. Now my face is as red as the kick ball, and I am all sweaty, and my hair is even more tangled than it usually is.

Oh, *perfect*.

I carry the ball over to Ms. Sanchez. "Hurry up," she says, scowling. She shakes the net bag.

And so even though the morning started out great, this has turned into the most terrible third-grade day I have ever had in my life so far. Because who cares about a special treat on Friday when the only friend you thought you had makes fun of you in front of everyone else?

In fact, they are probably all sitting in class and laughing about me and my weird room right now.

I just wish *I* had something to kick, that's all.

Like maybe—Cynthia Harbison.

❧ 3 ❧

тнinкing about my ugly room

I think animals are nicer than people. All you have to do is look around to know I'm right. Don't look around our condo, though, and expect to see any animals, because *"No Pets Allowed."*

But we didn't have any pets at our old house, even before we moved. My mom said it wouldn't be fair to them, because she was away at work all day long, and I was at school and then at child care until five-thirty every night.

I thought about getting a nocturnal pet, at least, like a possum or a skunk. "Nocturnal" means that the animals sleep during the day and run around all night, so it would have been perfect—except I guess Mom doesn't like either possums or skunks all that much, even though you can de-stink a skunk.

'Skunks can hear much better than they can see.

Supposedly.

My mom used to be a librarian for a big company, but then the company decided to get smaller. Lots of people lost their jobs and had to look for other work, including my mom. Now Mom works at home, correcting books that other people write. My father lives in England with his new wife, Annabelle, and no children. My parents got divorced when I was only two years old, but that's okay. I can barely even remember them living together.

I miss my dad, of course. He has come to visit me twice, but not with his wife. I've seen pictures, though. She looks okay, but she's not as pretty as Mom.

(And I'm not just saying that.)

"Guess what?" I say to Mom at dinner. "Our class is going to have a surprise treat on Friday afternoon. Parents are invited, too, Ms. Sanchez says."

We are eating sloppy joes and string beans, which is one of my favorite dinners, if you leave out the string beans.

"Really?" Mom says. "What kind of surprise treat?"

"I don't know. That's why it's a surprise," I explain patiently.

"Hmm," Mom says. "Well, you don't sound very excited about it, even though you've been complaining about how boring your new school is. In fact, you sound downright gloomy, Em."

"My new school *is* boring, compared to Magdalena," I say. "At Magdalena, we did tons of fun stuff. We even got to go out on a boat once, on that whale-watching trip. Remember?"

Mom sighs and nods at the same time. "I sure do," she says. "You got seasick, as I recall. You called me from the boat, from Janie McIntosh's cell phone, remember? You said to come and get you, because you were dying."

"Everyone got seasick on that trip," I remind my mom, coming to my own defense. "They didn't bring enough saltine crackers for all the upset tummies. But it was still fun."

"And it was expensive, too, as I recall," Mom says, remembering. "But I'll admit it—they did have a wonderful child-care program after school at Magdalena. Well, at least that's one thing we don't need anymore, now that I'm working at home."

"But I miss Magdalena," I say, trying not to whine. "I miss my friends. Don't you miss your friends from your old job?"

"Yes," Mom admits simply. "But so what? *They're* not there anymore, either. And your best friend at Magdalena moved to Arizona, don't forget," she adds. "So you wouldn't be seeing her, even if you still went there. But you still see some of your other old classmates from time to time, Emma."

"It's just not the same anymore," I say. I take a bite of my sloppy joe, which has gotten nice and soggy, just the way I like it. "Anyway, now I don't even *have* any friends," I mumble.

Mom takes a sip of her iced tea. "What about Cynthia Harbison?" she asks.

"She hates me. As of today," I inform my mom.

"Cynthia hates you?" Mom asks, setting down her glass of iced tea with a clunk. "But why? What happened?"

"Annie Pat Masterson was nice to me, that's what happened," I say. "She's the girl with red hair."

"I remember," Mom says, nodding slowly. "But—but why would that make Cynthia hate you, Emma? That doesn't make any sense."

"Try telling Cynthia that," I say. Then I take a big gulp of milk to wash down the bite of sloppy joe that suddenly feels as if it's stuck in my throat.

"Hmm," Mom says again. She spears a string bean with her fork and looks at it. "Maybe Cynthia is jealous of Annie Pat," she says. "Do you think?"

Jealous? That is the silliest thing I have ever heard. *Jealous* is for smoochy grown-ups in

love on TV, not for kids being friends at school—
or *not* being friends. "I don't think so," I say
politely.

Because I know that Cynthia was just feeling
mean, not jealous.

"Jealousy among friends happens all the
time," Mom says, looking as wise as a bee.

Bees
communicate
with each
other by
dancing and
buzzing.

I would say *As wise as an owl*,
except I think that bees are smarter.
They have a very intricate society.
We could learn a lot from bees.

"Oh," I say politely, still not
arguing with her. Because what's
the use? Things just happen. There
doesn't have to be a reason.

In fact, there usually *isn't* one.

Now Mom frowns. "So did you actually have
a fight with Cynthia?" she asks me.

"Kind of," I admit. "Not the kind of fight
where you punch each other, though. Just the
kind where I ended up all by myself on the play-

ground, having to pick up a kick ball that I didn't even play with."

I decide not to say anything about Cynthia making fun of my room. I don't want *Mom* to think I'm strange, too.

"Well, spending recess alone is bad enough," Mom says.

Thinking about my ugly room has given me an idea. "Can we go to the bookstore after dinner? I mean after we do the dishes?" I ask Mom. Because our local bookstore has all kinds of stuff in it besides books, things such as school supplies, art supplies, stickers—and posters.

Lots of posters.

Our bookstore barely has room for books anymore!

"Well, sure, I guess we can, if you don't have too much homework to do," Mom says after taking another sip of iced tea. She looks a little less worried now, and she has stopped asking me questions about Cynthia, thank goodness.

Mom loves going to the bookstore. It's always an easy way to distract her.

"Why do you want to go?" she asks me. "Do you need something special for school, honey?"

I nod my head and put my most serious expression on my face. "I do need something," I tell her solemnly. "I really, really do."

But it's not for school. I need posters of puppies and ducklings and birdies, that's what I need. Or newborn lions sucking on baby bottles, or kittens saying, *"Hang in there!"*

Anything cute—to put up in my room.

And I need those posters fast.

x 4 x

Ha-Ha on Cynthia

"Why are you wearing such a fancy dress?" Cynthia asks me the next day. It is Wednesday, which means only two more days until our treat. We are sitting down, waiting for class to begin. EllRay Jakes is standing next to Ms. Sanchez's desk, showing her a paper, so we are starting late.

"I'm wearing fancy shoes, too," I tell Cynthia, pointing a toe. I am wearing my shiny black too-small party shoes and white tights. I look like a girl today, that's for sure.

No one could possibly call me weird *or* strange.

My dress is lavender-blue, dilly dilly, just like the song says. Mom bought it for me six months ago, for Easter. The dress has tiny purple flowers on it, and it has a wide sash and about a hundred little buttons that go up the front. I could barely button them all up this morning. But it's okay, as long as I don't breathe.

Too much, I mean, or too deep.

I shrug, not answering Cynthia's question about why I am wearing this dress. "I wear stuff like this all the time," I fib instead, arranging my skirt so that it hides my knees. I scraped them last week, and the scabs are ruining the effect.

"No you *don't* wear dresses like that all the time," Cynthia informs me. She takes off her plastic headband, tucks her smooth, shiny hair behind her ears, then scrapes the headband back on her hair, pulling so hard that her eyes look surprised. "You hardly ever even wear dresses. You're just showing off," she says.

This makes me angry. "Ooh, I'm showing off for Cynthia-in-Wonderland," I say to her, pretending to smooth back my own hair. Alice in Wonderland wears a headband just like Cynthia's; that's the point of what I said. And Cynthia hates being teased, I know, so any joke on her is a good one.

Corey Robinson, who is sitting on the other side of me, starts to giggle. "Shut up, Freckle Face Corey," Cynthia says to him, leaning way across my desk.

Corey jumps back in his seat. He is a little bit scared of Cynthia, I think.

"Uh, excuse me," I say to Cynthia, pretending to be polite, "but you are trespassing on my property." I point down at my desk to make sure she knows what I mean. Of course by now, lots of kids are listening in. They are waiting to see what will happen next.

So am I.

"That desk is official school property," Cynthia says. "It's not private property. And so I am *not* trespassing. And anyway, you shouldn't call people names."

"Well, you called Corey a name," I remind her. "And you called me a name yesterday."

Next to me, Corey starts waving his hands

back and forth as if he is saying, *Hey, leave me out of this!*

"'Freckle Face' is not a name. It's a description. It's just the way he looks," Cynthia tells me.

Everyone sitting around us turns to inspect

poor Corey, who looks as if he is about to faint. All of his freckles—and he does have lots of them—seem to stand out like sprinkles of cinnamon on a sugar cookie.

"I could call him Freckle Face, or I could call him Seaweed Hair, and I *still* wouldn't be calling him names," Cynthia tells everyone. "I'd only be reporting, like they do on TV. It's just the way he looks," she says again.

Corey practices his swimming every day, see, and sometimes his yellow hair turns sort of green from the chlorine in the community pool. That's what Cynthia is talking about.

But he'll probably win a medal in the Olympics some day and be on the cover of *People*, so then who will be laughing?

"That's rude," this girl named Fiona says, although she is usually even shyer than I am. In fact, Fiona is so shy that she is practically invisible, but now, even Fiona is getting mad at Cynthia.

Cynthia looks around, kind of surprised to see that our own private fight has spread so far—and that she is losing.

"Yeah, that's rude, Cynthia," someone else says. "Corey didn't do anything to *you*."

"Well, I know he didn't," Cynthia says, turning pink. "It was all Emma's fault. She called me—" and Cynthia suddenly stops talking. I guess she doesn't want to say what I called her, in case kids remember it, and *they* start calling her that, too.

Corey takes a deep breath. "Emma called her 'Cynthia-in-Wonderland,'" he says. Then he lets all his air out, as if he is a runaway balloon. Only he doesn't go zipping around the room like a deflating balloon, he just shrinks back in his seat again.

All around us, kids are whispering, laughing, and nudging each other. And I am a little surprised. I only called Cynthia that because of her headband, but now that I think about it, Cynthia is a lot like Alice in the book.

The kids in my class must think so, too.

Cynthia and Alice are both very smooth and perfect to look at, for instance, and both girls can be bossy and grouchy. And Cynthia and Alice don't always see the funny side of things, even when there is a funny side staring you right in the face.

They are alike in good ways, too, even though I don't point out any of these good ways to the other kids. But Cynthia and Alice both have a lot of common sense, for example, and if Cynthia ever fell down a rabbit hole, she would instantly jump to her feet when she got to the bottom, just the way Alice did.

I would want to be friends with Alice, just like I wish I were still friends with Cynthia.

But I don't know how to turn this squabble around.

"Emma? Miss McGraw? Miss Emma McGraw?" Ms. Sanchez is saying. Uh-oh, she is halfway through taking attendance, and I didn't even hear her start.

"Oh. Here," I say.

"You look extra nice today, Emma," Ms. Sanchez says, pausing in her roll-taking. "Are you going to a special event after school that you'd like to tell us about?"

"No," I tell her, my heart pounding. "This is just a regular day, and I'm just wearing a regular dress, the same kind I always wear." Ms. Sanchez is making me nervous, though, and I try to squirm a little inside my so-called regular dress—except it is too tight for even a small-sized squirm.

Next to me, Cynthia snickers, and I change my mind about wanting to be friends with her again.

Ms. Sanchez tilts her head in a wondering

way, but she doesn't ask me any more questions. She continues taking roll.

Phew, I think—that was a close one.

And I try to curl my toes inside my party shoes. But I can't.

My feet feel hot, and they hurt. This is going to be a long, long day.

Oh well, I think, at least something good will happen *after* school. Because Annie Pat is coming over to my house to play!

My mom and I invited her last night.

So ha-ha on Cynthia.

x 5 x

Cute

"And here's my bedroom," I say to Annie Pat. I swing open the door.

Things are looking very different in here from the way they did yesterday at this time. There are no more pictures of grasshopper-chomping lizards, and no more skinks or skunks or sharks with a zillion teeth, or laughing hyenas. Who don't really laugh, in case you didn't know.

Now there are just three posters on the walls, and that's all. The first poster shows a baby chimpanzee wearing a diaper.

Cute.

The second poster is of a pile of kittens sleeping in a basket full of laundry that you just know is folded and clean.

Cute.

And the third poster shows a gray dog dressed up like Cinderella. I feel sorry for the dog, but the poster is definitely cute. All of my posters are cute. They should be! They cost me all the birthday money I was saving.

I told Mom it was time for a change.

"So, what do you think?" I ask Annie Pat, while I am also kicking off my stupid party shoes, which I will never wear again. I have been staggering around like a clown on stilts ever since lunch, which is when my feet started to feel as if they were about to fall off and limp to the emergency room all by themselves.

I sit down on the rug and peel off my tights, too. But I do that sort of sneakily, because my tights are so dirty and sweaty by now that they

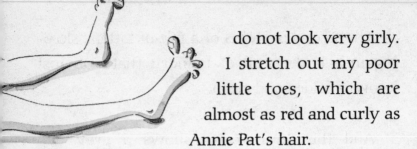

do not look very girly.
I stretch out my poor
little toes, which are
almost as red and curly as
Annie Pat's hair.

My toes are definitely not cute this afternoon.

Annie Pat looks around. "It's different from what I expected. It's not like Cynthia said," she tells me, shaking her head a little. Her curly red hair jiggles when she does this. She looks kind of disappointed. I wonder why?

"Well, sometimes I change a few things around. I redecorate," I say, being a little bit honest.

Hah—I have really changed a *lot* around. I took all of my old posters down, and I hid my shoe boxes full of shells, geodes, fossils, feathers, and cocoons. They are all in separate boxes of course, or else the fossils would get mixed up with the geodes, the cocoons would get smashed, and the feathers would get bent. But

I'm okay as long as Annie Pat doesn't search my closet.

For that reason, I decide not to change out of my party dress. My used-to-be party dress, I mean. No more celebrations for *this* outfit!

"What do you want to play?" Annie Pat asks me.

"Let's have a snack first," I tell her. My stomach is gurgling like anything, and that is definitely not very cute. "My mom is making us quesadillas," I tell Annie Pat.

"Yum," Annie Pat says, looking excited for the first time all afternoon.

We wash our hands and then hurry into the kitchen. Mom is cooking and reading some pages from her work at the same time, which usually means disaster. "I think you should turn those quesadillas over now," I tell her, looking at the hot griddle on the stove.

"Oh, okay," Mom says, surprised. "Why don't you pour some juice or some milk?"

She has already gotten out the fancy wine glasses, the way we talked about this morning.

"Ooo, pretty," Annie Pat says, picking one of the glasses up carefully. "We get to use *these*?"

"Sure," I say, shrugging as if it is nothing. Mom and I sneak each other a secret look, and I can't help but smile. I finish pouring the milk into the wine glasses while Mom cuts the quesadillas into triangles and puts them on our plates. The *good* plates, the wedding present ones that look as if there are beautiful, bumpy flowers growing all around their edges.

It would almost be worth getting married just to get plates like that.

"Ooo," Annie Pat says again, her eyes wide.

After our snack, we go back into my room to play. "I've got dolls," I tell Annie Pat, and I point to the shelf where I keep them. I have four good ones, and I also have lots of outfits for them, because that's an easy present for people to figure out, I guess. My mom says it's a kindness to relatives when there's something obvious they can buy for a kid.

"Cool," Annie Pat says, taking one of the dolls down. "Want to dress them up for a big party?"

"Yeah, or for school," I say. "For a special treat at school." We settle down on the rug and spread all the doll clothes around us. They really are pretty, and the little dresses and capes and pants look like tropical flowers that have fallen onto the floor.

It would be fun if we could play Amazon rain

forest, instead of dolls, but you can't have
everything.

I give my own scrunched-up lavender party
dress a tug.

Ugh. It's getting itchy.

"So, who do you think is prettier?" Annie Pat asks me. "Ms. Sanchez, or Barbie?"

I think about it for a minute. "Mmm, Barbie," I finally say. "Only Barbie's not real."

"I know," Annie Pat says, nodding. "And she's not engaged, either, if you don't count Ken." She reaches for a weensy pair of tiger-striped leggings.

"I never count Ken. But I wonder who Ms. Sanchez is getting married to?" I say. "Maybe it's some man from our school."

The doll droops in Annie Pat's hand. "Oh, I hope not," she says. "I mean, who would be handsome enough for her to marry?"

We both stop and think for a couple of minutes.

No, we finally decide, none of the men at Oak Glen Primary School would be right for Ms. Sanchez. "Maybe it's EllRay Jakes," I finally joke, giggling.

"Or Jared Matthews," Annie Pat says. She

pretends to be Jar-Head: "Hey, Ms. Sanchez—I *love* you," she bellows in that special Jared way.

"Settle down, Jared darling," I yell back to her, pretending to be Ms. Sanchez. "And please take your seat."

Annie Pat and I both crack up. "*Yahhh*," she finally gasps, holding her sides.

I notice that I have popped a couple of tiny buttons from laughing. The front of my dress is pooching open a little. "I guess I'd better go change," I say, getting up.

"Hey, I know what! We can dress *you* up, instead of the dolls," Annie Pat says, excited. "I'll go and get some clothes out of your closet."

"No, wait," I cry out, but it is too late—Annie Pat has opened my closet door.

And out tumble two of the shoeboxes.

And there are rocks and shells all over the floor.

Not only that, but a roll of my old nature pictures falls out, too.

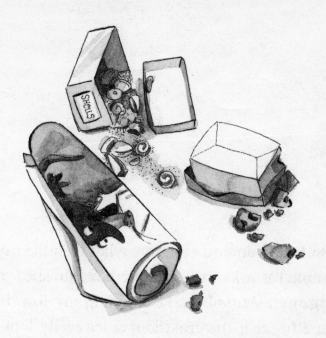

And the picture right on top shows—yeah, that's right: the stupid picture shows the stupid lizard eating the stupid grasshopper.

Annie Pat turns to stare at me.

✗ 6 ✗

Weird

"But why do you even *care* what Cynthia says?" Annie Pat asks me, after we have finished picking up my fossils and examining my lizard picture to see if the grasshopper leg really looks as if it is moving.

"Because she's my friend, that's why," I say. "Or she used to be."

"But she called you weird and strange, and in front of everyone, too," she reminds me.

"Maybe I am weird and strange," I say gloomily.

"Well, you're not *so* weird," Annie Pat says.

"Plus, I like nature just as much as you do."

"Really?" I say. "What kind of nature?"

"Underwater things, mostly," Annie Pat tells me. "I want to be an underwater scientist when I grow up. I plan to study the beaked sea snake. They're highly poisonous," she adds, looking important.

"Me, too," I say, excited now. "I mean, I'm not highly poisonous, but I want to be a nature scientist, too. Not the beaked-sea-snake kind, though—I'm not copying you."

"I know you're not," Annie Pat says, nodding loyally. "You would never copy."

I look over at my dolls. "But I like playing dress-up with dolls, too," I tell Annie Pat. Because if we are going to be friends, we might as well be honest with each other.

Beaked sea snakes are among the most venomous snakes on earth!

"Me, too," Annie Pat says. "I

think you can be a scientist and still like cute clothes."

"Yeah," I say, but then I sigh. "I wish she wouldn't call me names, though."

"Who, Cynthia?" Annie Pat says, laughing. "She called me 'Bozo' all last year, and we're still friends. Sort-of friends, anyway."

"She called you Bozo?" I ask, confused.

"Yeah. You know, like that old cartoon character Bozo the Clown," Annie Pat says. "The red hair," she explains, fluffing up her curls. "All the kids called me that, after she did. For a while, anyway."

"That wasn't very nice," I say, a little bit shocked. *Wow*, I think—second grade at Oak Glen Primary School must have been rough!

"Anyway," I say, "you don't look like a clown. You look very nice."

"Thank you," Annie Pat says.

"But how come Cynthia did that to you?" I ask Annie Pat.

"I don't know. She got mad about something," Annie Pat says, shrugging. "Something little."

"But that's no fair," I tell Annie Pat. "I mean, Cynthia called poor Corey 'Freckle-Face,' and he really hated it. You can't just go around calling people names. Names like—like 'Jar-Head,'" I say, giggling at the mean name I invented.

I can't help it!

Annie Pat wrinkles up her face, thinking. "Jar-Head? Oh, *Jared*. I get it," she says, and she laughs. "And don't forget 'Cynthia-in-Wonderland,'" she says.

"I know, but that was a good one. Almost a compliment," I tell her. "It's not like calling Fiona 'Baloney,' or something," I say, getting silly now.

"Yeah, or like calling EllRay 'Shrimpy,' because he's so short," Annie Pat says.

"Hey, watch it," I tell her, pretending to be mad. "I'm almost as short as he is."

"Oops! Sorry," Annie Pat says with a giggle. And we both crack up again.

"Or—or you could call Cynthia 'Bossy Pants,'" I say at last, after I have caught my breath. "That's a whole lot worse than 'Cynthia-in-Wonderland.' And how would she like that?"

"'Bossy Pants,'" Annie Pat says, trying it out in her mouth.

"How would *she* like it?" I ask Annie Pat again.

"Yeah, how would *she* like it?" Annie Pat asks me back.

We look at each other. One smile seems to zip back and forth from my mouth to Annie Pat's mouth, and you can hear my Felix the Cat clock ticking.

x 7 x

that's just tough!

Mom crunches a bite of toast and then looks at me. It is Thursday morning, which means that there is only one day left until our class treat. "What are you going to wear to school tomorrow?" she asks me.

"Ms. Sanchez says it has to be play clothes," I say, and I frown. I slosh my orange juice back and forth in the glass, pretending that we are having an earthquake, and I wonder if I have any play clothes that look girly enough. Because no way am I going to give Bossy Pants Cynthia a chance to make fun of me again.

Not tomorrow, when we will have our treat,

and not today, when Annie Pat and I are going to do our best to teach her a lesson.

"Well, you'd better decide now what you want to wear tomorrow," Mom says. "It took you way too long to get dressed this morning, Emma. We can't go through that again. And I need to make sure the clothes you want to wear will be clean."

"Okay. What about my pink T-shirt and white shorts?" I say to Mom, deciding fast. "And Band-Aids for my knees. But I want the cute kind with flowers on them, not the plain old skin kind. Even though I have never met anyone with skin that color. And could you wash my

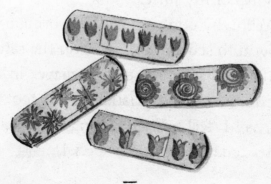

sneakers so they don't smell funny? And my white socks, too? They're in the hamper."

"All right," Mom says, sighing. "At least shorts and sneakers will be an improvement over what you've got on today."

What in the world does she mean? Today I am wearing my second-best shoes, not my regular sneakers. And I am wearing a plaid skirt and dark green sweater, even though it has been kind of hot out lately.

October can be sweltering in California.

"You're going to broil, sweetheart," Mom says, eyeing my sweater.

"Nuh-uh," I say, after taking a slow and dainty sip of my juice.

"Well, why don't you at least bring a T-shirt with you to school, just to be on the safe side?" Mom suggests. She is a big believer in always being on the safe side. Usually I am, too. But the thing is, I feel *safer* wearing my skirt and sweater today. I feel more special.

They match, like in a newspaper ad.

Still, I have a jangly feeling in my stomach when I think about Cynthia, and about the lesson that Annie Pat and I are going to teach her. I push my cereal bowl away and shake my head *no*.

Mom sighs. "Okay," she says, "only don't call me from school today, saying you've changed your mind and want me to bring you something more comfortable to wear. Because I've got a ton of work to do."

"I won't," I promise her.

I'm going to be far too busy to be making any *Mommy-help-me* phone calls today.

x x x

Annie Pat and I meet under the pepper tree in front of school, just the way we planned. She is wearing her second-best clothes today, too. "Okay," I tell her. "Now, I'll say it to Corey, and you'll say it to Heather. Okay?"

"Okay," Annie Pat says. She giggles way up

high, because of hearing all of our *okays*, maybe, and her face turns pink the way it does when Ms. Sanchez calls on her. "I'm scared," she whispers to me as we walk into class.

"Me, too, but so what?" I whisper back. "It'll serve Cynthia right for being so mean to us."

"Yeah, it'll serve her right," Annie Pat agrees, nodding her head up and down so fast that her curly hair bounces.

I sit down at my desk and try to tug my plaid skirt over my scabby knees.

Corey flops down in his seat, too, just as Cynthia prances into the room. She is not wearing her usual Wonderland headband today, I notice. "Hi," Corey says to me, then he looks at my skirt and sweater. "Are you going ice skating after school or something?" he asks.

See, there is an indoor rink at the shopping mall. That's what he's talking about.

But why can't people just mind their own business? I don't say that to Corey, however. He'd probably faint if I did. Even his freckles would faint! Instead, I say, "Not really," which doesn't make very much sense, once I think about it. People are either going ice skating, or they are *not* going ice skating. There is nothing in between.

"Oh," Corey says, looking confused.

Cynthia plops down into her seat and gives me a dirty look. She has probably heard that Annie Pat came over to my house after school yesterday.

Well, that's just tough! Let her be mad.

Across the room, I can see Annie Pat whisper something to Heather, and they both look at Cynthia and giggle. Next to me, Cynthia frowns a little and twiddles with a pencil.

I am going to have to hurry if I want to keep up with Annie Pat. "Hey," I whisper to Corey, "I wonder if Bossy Pants is going to yell at you again today?"

There, I've said it to someone in class—and so has Annie Pat.

Bossy Pants.

Pretty soon, everyone in class will be calling Cynthia that. At least I hope they will!

But Corey Robinson is confused. "Bossy Pants?" he asks in a very loud voice.

"Shhh. *You* know," I mutter to him, and I jerk my head in Cynthia's direction.

Cynthia tries to flip her hair back out of her eyes and looks as if she wishes she had worn a headband today, after all.

"Oh, yeah. *Her*," Corey mutters back, and he puts a hand over his mouth to hide a snorty laugh.

He nudges his neighbor and whispers something to her.

And Ms. Sanchez starts to take attendance.

We did it!

x **8** x

i'm Just Nervous, тнат's аLL

By lunchtime, everyone in the third grade is calling Cynthia "Bossy Pants," only behind her
back, not to her face. We're all too chicken to
say, "Hi, Bossy Pants! You sure are a Bossy
Pants," to the front of her. So we say it behind
her back, so Cynthia can't yell at anyone—even
though she knows that something strange is
going on.

And I am not feeling as wonderful as I thought
I would about the whole thing, only I can't
exactly explain why. Maybe it's because I don't
think it was very brave to make up a hurtful
name behind someone's back. Or maybe it's the

name itself. Because what does "Bossy Pants" mean, anyway? Nothing, that's what. How can pants be bossy?

For some reason, that name made more sense when I first invented it.

Or maybe I feel not-wonderful because Cynthia looks so sad. She has been slumped over her desk all morning, ever since nutrition break. Her mouth is turned down as if somebody drew it that way with a pink Magic Marker.

Even her *hair* looks droopy.

I know for sure that by now, she has heard what everyone is calling her. I only hope she doesn't know how that name got started, because now, I really don't know how to turn my fight with Cynthia around.

Our quarrel is kind of like an airplane that has already taken off.

"I guess *we* taught Cynthia a lesson, all right," Annie Pat says to me as we walk out to the playground. She doesn't sound very happy, though. Maybe *she* feels rotten about this whole thing, too.

"Yeah," I say, but I sound like a robot. "And I know what we taught her, too. We taught her that you can't trust your friends."

Annie Pat ducks her head as if I just spritzed her with a red plastic squirt gun. "Well," she says, "she had it coming, didn't she? *Didn't* she?" I can tell by the way she asks this question that Annie Pat really feels terrible about making Cynthia so sad.

Just the way I do.

"I can't remember," I say. "I know. Let's go ask Cynthia if she wants to eat lunch with us."

I actually feel sorry for Cynthia.

"She'll probably say no," Annie Pat say, scurrying behind me.

Gloomy Pat. That would be a better nickname

for Annie Pat today than Bozo, even though her hair is still curly and red.

And people could call me Mean Emma, I think, blushing a little bit. Or Emma-Wemma-Meanie. Or Emma-Meanie-Weenie.

"Hey, Cynthia, wait up," I say, hurrying to join her. She and Fiona are walking toward the shady bench by the chain-link fence. I guess Cynthia has forgiven Fiona for calling her rude, the same way that she probably would have forgotten all about the Cynthia-in-Wonderland thing, if Annie Pat and I hadn't gone and messed things up.

See, that's a *good* thing about Cynthia—she doesn't ever stay mad very long.

Until now, maybe.

A drop of sweat slides down the side of my face. My mom was right, it's way too hot to be wearing a sweater. I can feel trickles of sweat creeping down my back, too.

Oh, why didn't I just wear my regular clothes?

And why couldn't it have just been a regular day today, with regular Cynthia, regular Annie Pat, and regular Emma?

Too late.

Cynthia turns around, only instead of looking mad, she gives Annie Pat and me a one-corner smile. "Oh, hi," she says softly.

"Hi," Annie Pat says, catching up. "Hi, Fiona."

"Hi," Fiona practically whispers, and then she sits down, opens her lunch sack, and pulls out— a baloney sandwich!

I can barely believe my eyes, because I made up the name "Fiona Baloney" just last night. Thank goodness nobody heard *that* one—no one except Annie Pat, I mean.

Annie Pat has just spied the baloney sandwich, though, and she bites her lower lip to keep snirts of laughter from popping out of her mouth. Her face is almost as pink as Fiona's baloney.

Annie Pat stares down at the hot cracked playground asphalt as if it is the most interesting thing she has ever seen.

"Hi, Fiona," I echo. "Can we eat lunch with you guys?"

"Sure," Cynthia says, answering for Fiona. She looks around. "Where's Heather, anyway?" she asks.

"I think I saw her going to the cafeteria," Annie Pat announces. She looks as if she is glad to have something ordinary to say.

"Huh," Cynthia says, scowling. "Well, who even cares?" She makes a little face and brushes some dust off her pants.

Off her *bossy* pants.

I bite my lower lip, just the way Annie Pat did a minute ago—only I don't exactly feel like laughing.

I guess I'm just nervous, that's all.

"So, what's new?" Annie Pat says, poking around in her lunchbox. She still hasn't looked up.

"Oh, someone has been calling me really mean names, that's all," Cynthia says, a wobble in her voice. "For no reason," she adds, sniffing.

"No reason," Fiona says, like someone closing the same door twice.

"Huh," Annie Pat says, and she pulls out a sandwich bag and squints at it suspiciously. *Hey, she seems to be saying, maybe this sandwich bag started the whole thing!*

"And I'm going to find out who started calling me Bossy Pants if it takes me the rest of my life," Cynthia announces, and she nips off a corner of her sandwich like the fiercest snapping turtle in the world—worse than the one I saw on this show on PBS.

Snapping turtles can live to be 100 years or more.

I even used to have a picture of a snapping turtle up in my room.

Once upon a time.

"She'll find out if it takes her the rest of her life," Fiona echoes, nodding sharply. Finally, Fiona has found something to say—even if Cynthia said it first. *"Bossy Pants,"* Fiona says scornfully.

Annie Pat says, *"Gulp,"* just the way they do in cartoons. And she hasn't even started eating her lunch yet.

"You don't have to keep repeating that stinky name," Cynthia tells Fiona.

"I only meant that it's awful," Fiona says, almost fainting on the bench because of Cynthia's scolding.

"It's not awful, it's dumb," Cynthia corrects her. *Snap, snap!* "It's dumb, and it's mean, and it's just plain wrong. Do you think I'm bossy?" she asks Annie Pat, whipping her head around so fast that her shiny hair swings like a curtain.

"Mmph," Annie Pat says, panic in her eyes.

"Well, what about you, Emma?" Cynthia says, turning to face me. She is angry now. She is practically sending out sparks! "Do *you* think I'm a bossy pants?" she asks me.

I take a deep breath, then let it out with a whooshy noise. "Yeah, I do, kind of," I say.

Hearing my words, Cynthia is so surprised that she drops her peanut butter-and-jelly sandwich on the ground. Then her eyes get skinny and mean, and she says, "It was you, wasn't it? It was *you.*"

It's not a question the second time she says it.

9

So Busted

"I'm telling on you, Emma," Cynthia says to me. "I'm telling, and you are going to be in a lot of trouble. You are so *busted.*"

"Go ahead and tell," I say back. But my heart is pounding, *thunka-thunka-thunk.* I don't look at Annie Pat even for a second. Why get her in trouble, too?

Cynthia hooks her hair back over her ears with both hands. "You did it just to be mean," she says. "For no reason!"

"Yeah, for no reason," Fiona echoes in her shadow voice.

"Because I am *not* bossy," Cynthia informs

me. Her hands are on her hips now, and she looks like the Queen of Bossy to me.

"Oh, let's not get carried away, Cynthia," I say, which is actually something my mom says to me fairly often. Only she calls me *Emma*, not *Cynthia*, of course. "You try to make everyone do what you want them to, don't you? And that's what bossy is," I tell her. "So I did too have a reason."

Cynthia is outraged. "I do not make people do what I want," she says. "How would I do that?"

"By making fun of them, for one thing," I say. "Like the way you called me weird in front of everyone yesterday, just because I was starting to make friends with Annie Pat, and it wasn't your idea. You were trying to boss us then, weren't you?"

Annie Pat moans a little. I can tell that she does not want to be in the middle of this fight. She is trying to blend into the chain-link fence, and I don't blame her.

"Who cares what you do with your new best friend?" Cynthia asks me. "Anyway, you *are* weird. Just look at you," Cynthia says to me. "You're all bundled up in sweaters on the hottest day of the year."

"Yeah," Fiona says, trying to come up with a sneer. "Sweaters."

"It's just one sweater, and I'm only wearing it because it was cold when I got dressed this morning," I lie.

How can I tell Cynthia that something told me I needed to wear my second-best outfit today, and that just happened to be this skirt and sweater? After what she said about my bed-room, I wanted to make sure I really, really looked like a girl.

And a skirt definitely helps make that happen.

Anyway, today was supposed to be the spe-cial day that Annie Pat and I taught Cynthia a lesson about calling people names . . .

. . . by calling her a name.

So I *had* to get dressed up.

But how can I tell Cynthia that I was sorry about calling her "Bossy Pants" almost as soon as I had done it?

I can't, that's all. It is too hard to explain.

Even *I* don't understand it.

Cynthia sniffs. "You are so busted," she repeats. Then she looks down at her sandwich, which is still lying on the ground, of course. Because sandwiches can't just walk away, no matter how much they might want to.

I pick it up for Cynthia and try to brush it

off. "Here," I say, holding it out. "I think it's still good."

"My delicious sandwich is wrecked, and it's all your fault," Cynthia says, knocking the gritty sandwich out of my hand. "So now I'm going to starve."

Oh, sure. Starve.

Cynthia should get an award for Best Actress on a Playground, or something.

"I'll share with you, Cynthia," Fiona tells her, kissing up like crazy. She holds out what is left of her baloney sandwich.

Fiona is starting to get on my nerves. I think I liked her better when she was invisible.

"Thanks, but no thanks," Cynthia says, eyeing the pink lip of baloney that is hanging out of Fiona's sandwich. "Come on, Fiona—let's go find Ms. Sanchez so we can tell on Emma."

And off they march: *Hup*-two-three-four.

I look at Annie Pat, and Annie Pat looks at me. "Yow," Annie Pat says. Her face is so white now that she really *does* look a little like a clown. The sad kind, though.

"Yeah, yow," I agree. My heart has stopped thunking, but I am still sweating. It's probably because of the sweater, though.

We finish eating our lunches as slowly as

possible and then zigzag back to class just before the bell rings. Ms. Sanchez is busy writing something in a notebook. Her engagement ring twinkles as her hand moves across the page.

Cynthia is already sitting at her desk with her hands folded and her chin up in that stubborn, *Told-you-so!* way she has.

Uh-oh.

Fiona shoots me a look that says, *Serves you right.*

I give *her* a look that says, *Shut up, Fiona Baloney.* But I don't say it out loud.

Most of the other kids look sleepy after stuffing themselves full of lunch on such a hot day. But then, our class is usually drowsy after lunch, I have noticed. Ms. Sanchez almost has to blow a police whistle to get our attention.

Luckily, she has one—and she knows how to use it.

Jared and EllRay are managing to shove each other around, in spite of being inside the classroom. "Move it," Jared mutters, whomping EllRay with his shoulder. "Get out of my face."

I can't tell whether they are joking or not. The kids standing next to them cringe out of the way. They don't *care* if it's a joke.

Even if someone is laughing when they sock you, it still hurts, doesn't it?

"Make me move, Hulk," EllRay bellows. You would be surprised at how loud his voice is for such a little guy. He rams Jared with his head as if Jared were a big old soccer ball.

Which he isn't, of course.

Jared says, *"Oof!"* and then he says, "Don't call me names, Shrinky."

Shrinky! That's an even better name for EllRay than "Shrimpy" is, I think.

But I guess Ms. Sanchez doesn't think so, because—she slams her notebook shut, flings down her golden ballpoint pen, and jumps to her feet. "I have had just about enough," she announces.

And the whole world stops.

x 10 x

You WiLL Not BeLieve tHis

Everyone is frozen, just like in a game of Statues.

"Take - your - seats," Ms. Sanchez says. Her voice sounds as though it is made out of ice cubes, her words are so cold and hard.

All the kids who are still standing fling themselves into their seats, and there is a little *murmur-murmur-murmur* of concern and excitement.

"Quiet," Ms. Sanchez commands us, raising one hand, and we are quiet. Just like that.

And then Corey Robinson, who is sitting next to me, makes the teensiest peeping noise you have ever heard. In fact, I am probably the only one who can hear it. I bite my lips together so I don't giggle in that horrible way that happens sometimes exactly when you don't mean it to.

"Thanks a lot, *Jared*," somebody mutters, because it is natural for our class to blame Jared when something goes wrong. It's kind of a habit.

"Quiet," Ms. Sanchez says again, slapping her desk with her engagement hand this time.

Ow. That must have hurt, I think. She must really be mad.

Ms. Sanchez looks down at her desk as if she's surprised that it is still there. Then she sweeps her look across the room as if it is a flashlight that is searching for bad guys— but it shines on everyone in the class.

"I have had just - about - enough," she repeats. "And it's going to stop - right - now." She is snapping out each word.

I'm not sure what she has had just about enough *of*, but I am not about to ask any questions. And anyway, I think we are all about to find out.

So I sit here and wait.

"I don't know what's wrong with you people," Ms. Sanchez says, "calling each other names the way you've been doing lately."

Oh.

And she called us *"you people."* Frowning heads swivel to look at Jared and EllRay, who were the most recent name-callers.

"It's not just them," Ms. Sanchez tells us. "It's not just Hulk and Shrinky, over there. Think about it," she says. "Bossy Pants? Porky? Bozo? Skinny Bones? Freckle Face? Cynthia-in-Wonderland? Do those mean names ring any bells?"

I can feel myself blush. Boy, she doesn't miss much.

I'm just glad she doesn't know about "Jar-

Head" and "Shrimpy" and "Fiona Baloney."

I know who most of those names are, all right. But who is Porky, and who is Skinny Bones? I can't help but wonder.

"You can call anyone an unkind name," Ms. Sanchez is saying. "It's the easiest thing in the world to do."

I think that breathing is easier, and blinking, and eating chocolate cake is *definitely* easier, but I see what she's getting at.

"Calling names is also boring," Ms. Sanchez informs us, "and it's lazy, and just plain mean. So class, do you want to just sit around making up hurtful names for each other all year long?" Ms. Sanchez asks us.

Everyone kind of peeks around, afraid that someone is going to be dumb enough to raise a hand to answer that question. Will Heather say, *"Oh, oh!"* the way she usually does, and wave her arm around so she will be the number-one person Ms. Sanchez calls on?

No. Even Heather has figured out that Ms. Sanchez is not really waiting for an answer, we are all relieved to see.

"Because if you are going to be busy calling each other names, and making mischief, then we certainly won't have time for any special treats," Ms. Sanchez continues.

Oh no, we are all thinking at once.

You can almost hear our voices.

Ms. Sanchez waits, for the count of three. *One – two – three.*

And then she says, "Well? Does anyone have anything they'd like to say to me, and to the class?"

And you will not believe this, but I can feel myself standing up.

Me, Emma McGraw.

The second-shortest kid in the third grade.

The newest kid in the third grade.

Every bone in my body is quaking, but I guess they all still work, because I am finally—

after what feels like about a year—on my feet. "I have something to say," I croak to Ms. Sanchez.

I can hear Corey make his peeping noise again. Obviously, he can't stand even sitting *next to* a person who is in so much trouble.

"Yes, Emma?" Ms. Sanchez says. She looks very, very serious.

"I'm sorry that I called Cynthia 'Bossy Pants,'" I say. "And also, I'm sorry I called her 'Cynthia-in-Wonderland' yesterday," I add. Then I sit down, right before I fall down.

There is a roaring sound in my ears, but I can tell that someone else has stood up, too. It's EllRay Jakes! "I'm sorry I

called Jared a hulk," he says.

Even *Jared* is standing up. "And I guess I'm sorry I called you 'Shrinky,'" he tells EllRay.

"And I'm sorry I called Emma weird," someone is saying. "She isn't, not really. Not *so* weird, anyway."

It's Cynthia.

My friend, Cynthia!

I duck my head as if I'm saying, *Thanks. That's okay.*

"I called Cynthia 'Bossy Pants,' too," Annie Pat says, standing up to confess. "But I didn't really mean it. I *like* her."

There is a little silence in the room. "Anyone else?" Ms. Sanchez asks us.

We all peek around again.

"Well, I guess that will have to do for now," our teacher says. "Get out your workbooks, please."

Our workbooks? *But what about our treat tomorrow?* we are all shrieking, only without making any noise. We look at each other, our eyes wide.

But Ms. Sanchez ignores our panicky expressions and our one silent question. "Page forty-two," is all she says.

❊ 11 ❊
the Dreaded phone tree

Later on, just after lunch, one kid finally dares to ask Ms. Sanchez about our treat. It's Heather. She raises her hand, but she doesn't say, "*Oh, oh.*"

Instead, she gets slowly to her feet and says, "Um, should we still wear our play clothes to school tomorrow?"

"That's always a good idea, Heather," Ms. Sanchez says, not looking very interested in the question. She isn't giving anything away.

But Heather is braver than I thought. She doesn't sit down. Instead, she asks *another* question. "Well, what about our parents? Should they still come to school tomorrow afternoon with their cameras?"

Wow, Heather is so smart! Ms. Sanchez will *have* to answer that question, because it involves parents. And parents count more than kids—at least with other adults.

It's as if they're all in the same secret club.

"Mmm, I'll have to think about that," Ms. Sanchez says. "But don't worry. I'll let all the parents know tonight what's going on—*everything* that's been going on—through the phone tree."

Uh-oh. The dreaded phone tree.

See, we have one Room Mother, who is Mrs. Jakes. That's EllRay's mom. And if something important happens, Ms. Sanchez is supposed to call her on the phone, and then Mrs. Jakes is to call two other parents. Then those two parents call two more parents each. No parent will have to make more than two phone calls, but pretty soon everyone knows the important news, whatever it is.

And that is the phone tree, although nothing up to now has been important enough to use it.

(I still don't know why they call it a *tree*, though.)

All the kids in class are extremely worried to hear that Ms. Sanchez will be using the phone tree, of course—because that means our parents will know that something went wrong at school today.

In my opinion, that is our own private business.

In my opinion, using the phone tree for something like this is just plain *tattling*.

⚹ ⚹ ⚹

At home tonight, the phone rings only once. I think about grabbing it and yelling, *"Nobody home!"* and then hanging up, but Mom gets there first.

Afterward, my mother doesn't say one word to me about that phone call. And her face looks exactly the same way it always does when she tucks me in.

I give her an extra hug, though. Just because.

X X X

It is finally Friday morning, and I am wearing my pinkest T-shirt and my whitest shorts, just the way I planned. And they're a perfect mix of *cute* and *comfortable*, which I think will be my clothes policy from now on—unless I get an outfit that is extremely cute but *not* comfortable, in which case I will probably wear it anyway.

At least for short periods of time.

I am also wearing flowery Band-Aids on my knees. And I have on my pure white socks, and sneakers that still feel a little bit wet and heavy and cold from being washed last night. But they are clean, at least.

I look like a girl, all right. Not weird. And I even look fairly cute, although I don't know if we are going to have our special treat today or not.

When Ms. Sanchez takes attendance, we all sit up straight and say *"Here,"* in nice loud voices, except for EllRay, who says *"Present,"* just to be fancy. Everybody gives him a dirty look. But Ms. Sanchez doesn't say anything. She just continues to take roll.

If our class was on TV this morning, you could tune in and see a bunch of perfect kids in a perfect third-grade class.

Well, we aren't any better at math than we usually are when we try to do complicated long-number subtraction standing up at the board. But we are polite, and we talk one at a time, and we don't trespass on our neighbors' desks, and we don't keep asking to sharpen our pencils or to go to the bathroom.

We are trying very, very hard to be good.

Finally, it's nutrition break. "Did your mom say anything to you about this afternoon?" Cynthia asks me. She gives me a sweet, shy smile, which is the closest Cynthia Harbison is ever going to get to giving anyone an apology. She's just not built for backing down.

But that's okay. I like her anyway.

Cynthia has obviously decided to put our fight behind us, which is probably where it belongs. Putting bad things behind her without saying she's sorry is something Cynthia is known for doing—*after* she has said every hurtful thing that could possibly pop into her head, of course. I find it a little more difficult than she does to *"forgive and forget,"* as my mom sometimes puts it.

But, "Nuh-uh," I say back, shaking my head. "Did your mom or dad say anything to *you*?"

"My dad answered the phone last night, when Ms. Sanchez called," she tells me. "Only he didn't say anything afterwards. He just shook his head at me in his disappointed way."

When a grown-up shakes his head at you, especially *slowly*—that's a bad thing. "Uh-oh," I say.

Annie Pat passes around a little plastic bag filled with carrot strip curls. "I think all *we're* going to get this afternoon is *yelled at* again," she says between delicate, hamsterlike munches. "And that won't exactly be a surprise."

"Yeah," Heather agrees. "And then we'll get yelled at some more when we go home. They're just waiting," she adds grimly.

Fiona sighs.

After nutrition break, we go through our spelling words and take turns using them in sentences. And nobody tries to make up any funny sentences today, not even Jared.

As I said before, if you were watching us on TV, you would think we were perfect. And then you would probably change the channel, I guess, because what is so interesting about perfection?

When it is time for lunch, we all scurry to our cubbies, heads down. Ms. Sanchez still hasn't said anything. She's just sitting at her desk, reading an official-looking memo.

It looks as though there isn't going to be any treat.

So we drag ourselves out to the playground. "I'm not very hungry," Cynthia announces, looking tragic.

"Ooo, can I have your sandwich, then?" Heather asks her. Because by now, we have all discovered that Cynthia's father makes the best sandwiches of all the third-grade parents.

Cynthia sighs. "No," she says bravely, "I'm going to *try* to eat."

"Well, can I have half your sandwich?" Heather asks.

"What do you think our treat was going to be?" Annie Pat asks me, crunching down on a tortilla chip.

We have all been wondering about this for the last three days, of course. Heather was still hoping for a trip to the zoo. Fiona thought the treat would probably be relay races, or something like that. Maybe with prizes. And EllRay thought that Ms. Sanchez might pile us all into a bus, take us to Disneyland, and give us each a large sum of money to buy souvenirs with.

He tends to get a little bit carried away, but it's nice to have at least one optimist in the class.

"I thought we were going to have an ice cream party," I admit to Annie Pat. "You know,

with cones and sprinkles and stuff. Or with sweet gooey sauces and squirty whipped cream."

"We could have made a giant banana split—three feet long, maybe," Annie Pat says, getting as excited as if this were actually about to happen. "Yum."

"Yeah, yum. Only it's not true," I remind her.

We peek into our lunchboxes. I have squashed raisin cookies for dessert, and Annie Pat has a little container of applesauce.

Nope. It's not the same as even a one-foot-long banana split.

All the other Oak Glen kids are swarming around us as if they were an ant colony on the move, as usual, but Ms. Sanchez's class is eating a slow-motion lunch today. Every so often, somebody sighs. I smooth my pretty Band-Aids down over my knees, but no one gives me any compliments about them.

People are a lot faster to criticize you when you're a little bit weird and strange than they are to say something nice when you are a lot normal, in my opinion.

But then, just when the bell is about to ring, and about two minutes after we have finally given up hope, we hear an unusual noise.

Someone is blowing a whistle.

A whistle!

It is Ms. Sanchez, *our* Ms. Sanchez. Only now she is wearing play clothes, just like us—but neater. Tan pants, and a snug red T-shirt with the sleeves rolled up cute, and navy-blue sneakers.

And her engagement ring, of course.

And she is standing over by the side gate, the one that leads to the lawn.

We get to have our treat after all!

x 12 x

How Cool is That?

"Yay," we all shout. Our class likes to say *yay* every chance it gets.

We charge toward the gate like a herd of wildebeests and slam-dunk our lunch trash into the garbage can there. "*Yay-y-y!*"

Ms. Sanchez actually giggles as we churn through the gate and tumble onto the lawn.

See, at our school there is this big sloping lawn right next to the play-ground. We don't normally get to play there, though, because there is no fence around it. It is usually just a decoration lawn.

Wildebeests look like big antelopes with long beards.

But today, there is something that looks like a big silky puddle in the middle of the grass. It almost looks like an ice skating rink, only it can't be ice, because it is so hot out.

"Yay-y-y-y." Our cheers get softer and sound more puzzled as we get nearer to the puddle. But it's not a puddle, I see, it's cloth—a gigantic piece of shiny striped cloth that seems to bubble and ripple with excitement even though it is lying flat on the grass.

We creep up to it as though it were alive. Jared and EllRay are making muttery noises to each other as if they're planning how to whomp it if it gives anyone any trouble.

We spread out around the edges of the humongous cloth. Maybe our treat is under there, some of us are thinking.

Maybe it's pizza!

Ms. Sanchez blows her silver whistle once again, and we all jump a little. "Boys and girls," she calls out. "This is a parachute, a real parachute, and I've brought it for you to play with this afternoon."

Huh? A *parachute*?

"Well, I'm not jumping out of any trees," Corey announces to me, almost squeaking like a bat, he is so alarmed. He looks nervously up at the California live oaks that shade the far end of the lawn.

"Ooo, she must really be mad at us if she's going to make us use a parachute," Fiona says, keeping her voice low. Her eyes zip back and forth, as if she is planning her escape.

Has our teacher gone *nuts*?

Ms. Sanchez sees us fidgeting around, and she laughs a laugh almost as silvery as her whistle. "This parachute was donated to our school by my fiancé," she says proudly. "He and I go skydiving, sometimes," she adds, trying to sound casual.

Ms. Sanchez skydives with her boyfriend!

Cynthia, Annie Pat, and I exchange excited

glances. This is enough news to last us all year long, probably. She is talking about the man she is going to marry, the one who gave her the twinkly ring.

Her *fiancé.*

Corey, EllRay, and Jared stare at Ms. Sanchez, awed. Their jaws are practically hanging open, they are so impressed. A skydiving third-grade teacher!

How cool is that?

"He'll be joining us in a few minutes, and so will some of your parents," Ms. Sanchez says.

Nearby, Heather squeals, "Oh goody! He's coming." Heather is very romantic.

I'm just nosy. I want to get a look at this guy.

Jared raises his hand respectfully. "Uh, Ms. Sanchez?" he calls out. "How are we going to get the parachute up in the air? Is your—uh—your *boyfriend* bringing an airplane with him?"

Jared is afraid to say *"fiancé,"* I realize, and that makes me like him a little bit more.

Ms. Sanchez laughs again. "No," she says, "Mr. Timberlake will *not* be bringing an airplane."

Mr. Timberlake! Annie Pat and I look at each other and practically fall over with delight.

"But she can't marry Justin Timberlake," Corey Robinson mutters, worried. "He wouldn't make a very good husband for her. He has lots of girlfriends, doesn't he? And that's not a very good quality in a husband."

"It's not the same Mr. Timberlake, stupid," EllRay tells him.

"Shhh, don't call anybody any names," somebody warns.

"All right, listen," Ms. Sanchez calls out, ignoring our excited chatter. "I want you to spread out so that you're circling the parachute."

We straggle around the edges of the parachute until we look about even.

"Okay," Ms. Sanchez says, "now grab the edges."

Each one of us leans over and takes hold of some cloth. I am surprised at how strong it feels. You couldn't tear it with your hands, I think, no matter how hard you tried.

"Okay," Ms. Sanchez says again. "Now, we are going to count to three, and each time we count, I want you to lift the parachute up as high as you can. And when we finally say three, you can jump under the parachute."

This sounds a little strange to me.

"*Yay-y-y,*" a few kids shout, but the cheers sound feeble.

"Ready?" Ms. Sanchez asks us. "Okay. One . . . "

We hoist the parachute as far off the ground as we can. It feels heavy!

"Two . . ." we say together, starting to get excited.

"Three!" A whole bunch of arms toss the parachute as high in the air as it can go, and we all dive underneath before it can billow down to earth again.

"*Yay-y-y-y!*" someone squeals.

Hey, it's me!

Silky cloth begins to settle around us in poofy bubbles, and we plop down onto the cool green grass with striped silk falling all around us. It is

Pearls are created by living creatures called mollusks.

the most amazing feeling that I have ever felt! It is like being the grain of sand in the middle of a beautiful pearl.

Which is how pearls are formed, in case you didn't know.

Not with parachutes, of course, but with grains of sand.

Our entire world is grass and silk and filled with laughter.

Sun shines through the parachute cloth. Being under that striped silk is like playing inside a cloud, only better. We are in our own private little bubbles, but we are also together.

Somewhere, I can hear a whistle blow. "And again," Ms. Sanchez's tiny voice cries.

We crawl out from under the parachute, panting and laughing. Everyone's hair is all messed up and their clothes are grass-stained and twisted, but who cares?

Boy clothes and girl clothes, who *cares*?

By now, some grown-ups have gathered on the lawn. They are pointing and laughing, and a few of them are taking pictures. One dad even has a video camera.

I see Ms. Sanchez, and she is laughing, and holding some man's hand. He's not *Justin* Timberlake, but pretty close. He is very tall and blond, and as handsome as Annie Pat and I hoped.

And I think I see my mom. *Yippee!* I wave my arms at her until she waves back.

"Take hold of the parachute again," Ms. Sanchez calls out above our excited voices.

But we already know what to do, this time. "One . . ."

Up from the grass comes the parachute!

"Two . . ."

Higher in the air it goes.

"*Three-e-e-e!*" Onto the shadowed, glowing

lawn we dive. Annie Pat and Cynthia and Heather and Fiona and Corey and Jared and Stanley and EllRay and I, and all the other kids in class I haven't even made friends with yet.

The perfect smell of grass fills our noses, and stripey light fills our eyes as we grab sweaty handfuls of the parachute. We try to make the biggest, silkiest bubbles we can. I turn one way and bump into somebody warm, then I roll in another direction until I thunk into someone else. But with the parachute wrapped around me, I can't tell who is who. We are all the same.

My heart feels so light that I can almost see it rise up, up inside the parachute like a little pink balloon. *"Yay-y-y-y!"*

No more hurt feelings and squabbles. No more Hulky Shrimpy Shrinky Bozos. No more Porky Skinny-Bones Bossy-Pants Freckle-Faces, either.

And nobody is weird, especially not me.

For once, we are all exactly the same thing at exactly the same time.

Just kids!

From far away, the sound of our beautiful, in-love teacher's whistle floats across the wide blue sky, and I am just a plain old girl who is perfectly, perfectly happy.

For once.

But even once is pretty good, in my opinion.